Trevor's Shorts

Volume 1

Dr Trevor J Johnson

tjjch@hotmail.com

https://trevorjohnson.net

Trevor's Shorts

Volume 1

... they'll make you laugh, cry, angry, happy, sad ...

Trevor Johnson

Text copyright © 2019 Trevor Johnson
All rights reserved
ISBN 9781701533707

'Trevor's Shorts' is a collection of stories that I have written over the years: some for competitions, some because an idea occurred to me, and some just for fun. There's no real common theme: comedy, love, revenge, dark side, and prejudice are all here. Some are very short, some are longer.
  Happy reading.

Read more of the words I have written and tell me what you think at http://www.trevorjohnson.net

Table of Contents

The pregnant hamster

Most of the time we forget where we learnt something. But I'll always remember how I found out that you have to talk to a hamster that has recently given birth.

I worked for many years in a language school in Cambridge. It was a small school occupying one of those large Victorian houses on the North side of Parkers Piece. The students came from all over the world, with a preponderance from Eastern Europe. These were the sons and daughters of the nouveau rich. The parents had made their fortunes by being in the right place at the right time (or perhaps the wrong place at the right time, depending on the degree of legality) when the communist states went capitalist. They gave their kids everything they'd never had, resulting in arrogant adolescents, or to use the vernacular, spoilt brats.

I must have heard every reason for being late or missing classes. Some were believable, many were not. Some were stupid, many very clever. The 'A+' of excuses went as follows:

Two, young, Russian ladies arrived at the first break on a Monday morning.

"Good afternoon Sir."

"Good morning. Nice of you two to arrive, one hour late!"

"Yes, sorry for this." Said with about as much sincerity as a farmer would use when approaching the turkey three days before Christmas.

They looked at each other and back at me.

"Well? Is one of you going to explain to me or do I have to guess?"

Communism may have died, but the Russian suspicion of anybody asking too many questions, meaning more than one, lived on. From the expression on my face they obviously got the message that more explanation was mandatory.

"We go to Ely."

"Thank you, Natasha, that explains everything."

"No, you not understand."

"You're right, I do not understand."

"We go to Ely to take back hamster."

"Do you mean you are going, future, or you have already been, past?"

"We already ..."

"We have already ..."

"We have already been to Ely."

"Good, now we have the tenses right, what's this about a hamster?"

I really believed they couldn't understand why I wanted to know more.

"We ... I ... buy ... bought hamster ... a hamster in market in Ely on Saturday."

"Ah, so it's your hamster, Olga."

"Yes, Sir. On Sunday morning there is three ... "

"are three."

"are three hamsters in cage."

"Three?"

"Two babies."

"So, the hamster you bought was pregnant."

"Yes, we take back, make protest."

"We will have to do something about your tenses, Natasha."

"Please?"

"Never mind. You could have taken it back after class."

By the way droplets of perspiration started to appear on their foreheads, I could see that they really felt this was a KGB interrogation.

"No, market close at four."

"OK Olga, but if you bought the hamster, why did it need two of you to go to Ely and miss the first part of the class?"

Now they just exchanged glances that were a mixture of pity for me and amazement. If they'd said anything it would probably have been, 'are you stupid, or something?'

However, finally Natasha said, as if it was the most obvious thing in the world, "Olga drive car, and I hold cage and talk to hamster mother."

Coincidences

"Can you smell smoke?"

His more-than-a-whisper brought her back from the edge of unconsciousness. "What?"

"Can you smell smoke?"

"Smoke?"

"Yes, smoke."

"Where?"

"What do you mean 'where'? I don't know where."

His voice was even louder, and now she was fully awake. "Almost the first words you've said to me since last weekend, and you ask me if I can smell smoke!"

"Can you?"

"No."

"I was sure I could smell something." He reached out and switched on the bedside light.

"Do we have to have that on?"

"I want to know what that smell is."

"I told you we should have had those smoke detectors fitted when we had that special offer through your company, but you said no, in your usual stubborn way."

"I wasn't being stubborn."

"No?"

"No. Mary bought them and wasn't all that pleased. They went off almost at random, and the little, red, flashing lights were annoying. I found the one in the bedroom particularly irritating."

"Can we go back to sleep now?"

"Are you sure you can't smell something?"

"The only thing that smells around here is something fishy about your behaviour."

"We went through that last weekend, that's why we've hardly spoken since. I'll say it again, there's nothing 'fishy' as you put it."

"Some strange coincidences though."

"They do happen."

"Hmm."

"I'm getting up to have a look."

"Tell me again why you had to take Mary to the meeting last month."

He stopped with one leg out of bed. "You want to go through it again, do you?" He lay back down.

"No."

"Means yes. The meeting was the final negotiation and I wanted someone to take complete notes."

"You have Eric, your assistant."

"He'd been too involved so far."

"And he's not as sexy as Mary."

"I'll tell him you said that."

"To you I mean. I find him quite yummy."

"Yummy! I'll tell him you said that also. Sniff, sniff"

"So, what's the answer?"

"What's the question?"

"Mary and the meeting."

He sighed. "I wanted someone who would not be drawn into the discussions; Mary's my secretary, they'd met her

5

before so it didn't seem so strange, and she's one of the few people left who still take shorthand."

"All very convenient."

"If you want to see it that way."

"I don't, but it's difficult not to. In a hotel for three days and three nights–"

"Two nights actually."

"Two nights, three nights, what's the difference? One night's more than enough. Hard negotiations during the day, need to relax afterwards. What did you say you did in the evenings?"

Another sigh. "I told you, I had the financial team working here in the office and I spent most of the evening on the 'phone with them."

"All the more reason to relax afterwards. The warm, Mediterranean nights, difficult to sleep, even if that's what you wanted to do. Late supper overlooking the sea, lingering over coffee, the unspoken question and answer."

"You've got a vivid imagination. You should write a book."

"Perhaps you can help me with some of the details. Whose room for example?"

"I can still smell smoke," he started to get out of bed again.

"Getting a bit too close to the truth am I now?"

"No, I just don't want the house to burn down."

"So, what about Frank's house-warming party last week?"

This time one leg remained out of the bed. "You are determined to go through this all again."

"You woke me up."

"And given your lack of concern, I wish I hadn't."

"Once you've done something, you can't just 'wish you hadn't'."

"There must be a deeper meaning to that, but at this time of night it's gone completely over my head."

"You'd make it do that at any time of the day."

"If you say so."

"I do. Now, what about Frank's party?"

"Back to that."

"Yes, 'back to that'."

"I don't see how you think I could have planned anything with Mary. You were invited to Frank's party and only decided not to go at the last minute because of your migraine."

"Oh, I don't say you planned it, but when the opportunity arises …"

"You were the one who insisted that I go alone."

"I said just to put in an appearance for an hour or so, not until three thirty in the morning."

"What was that noise?"

"I didn't hear anything."

"I did. Something falling."

"Well I know what's not falling, and that's me for the story you told."

"Not a story, the truth."

"Oh, I'm sure parts of it are true, interwoven with some half-truths and some, what shall we call them, lies?"

"All the truth."

"That might just be another lie."

"I give up"

"Oh don't do that. That's almost like admitting you're guilty."

"Of what I don't know."

"OK, let's see, how did it go? Not so many people had turned up, so you felt a bit embarrassed about leaving quickly - I'm sure that's true."

He mouthed 'thank you'.

"You eventually left at eleven thirty - must be true because I could ask Frank."

"Go ahead."

"On the other hand you probably know I wouldn't because it might embarrass you - a double bluff."

"I've changed my mind about you being a writer, you should be a lawyer."

"You'd being driving for about 15 minutes when the car suddenly started misfiring and eventually stopped - possible, of course, but why it miraculously starts three hours later, and the garage can't find anything wrong is a mystery."

"They said it could have been something that temporarily blocked the fuel line."

"Which, as you know, is way beyond my limited knowledge of cars. You'd forgotten your mobile 'phone – true, it was on the hallway table, but that's something you've never done before; generally you spend more time talking to it than you do to me."

"I don't talk to the telephone, I talk to other people through it. I can still smell something. I want to check."

"Let me finish your story first. So there you are, in the middle of nowhere, not sure where you are because you've never been that way before. What to do? Start walking towards some distant lights, hoping to find a telephone to call the AA. After a few minutes the road ahead is lit up by a car coming up behind you. You're rescued! And, another miracle, it's Mary!"

"And I told you it was Mary. I could have said it was a stranger."

"You could have. I've thought about that. If I'd checked with Frank what time you left, and he just happened to mention it was a few minutes before Mary, I might have put two and two together."

"And got five!"

"No, that there was a good chance she would be the next car down that lonely, country road. Anyhow, you 'phone the AA on Mary's mobile, and she, very kindly, offers to stay with you until they arrive. Did you tell her you were afraid of the dark or something?"

"And what would you have done in the circumstances, just abandoned the person, I suppose?"

"If it was my boss and I was having an affair with him, no, too good an opportunity."

"Ah, so it's an affair now is it?"

"What would you call it?"

"There's nothing to call anything."

"We'll see, because now we get to the really difficult part of the story to believe. The AA, 'you just call out my name', 'you've got AA friend', never arrives. The two of you sit there for three hours. By chance you try to start the car and wonder of wonders it starts. What did you do during all that time? No, don't answer that, I don't want to know. Did she take some shorthand?"

"I told you, we listened to the radio most of the time, between repeatedly 'phoning the AA."

"Of course that's not checkable. They'd never admit, especially to me a non-member, that they didn't go to the rescue of a member. I suggested that you write a strong letter to them, but you said it wouldn't do any good."

"It wouldn't. Now, can I go and check downstairs before we are burnt alive?

"Hell's a fiery place for cheaters. You can go after the big question, which is, did any of this happen? OR did you and Mary leave Frank's within a few minutes of each other, meet up on the road, abandon your car, and spend the next few hours in her bed?"

"What an imagination."

"So it's not true?"

"Absolutely not, and that's the truth."

"Ah, but which do you mean, your story or my imagination?

"You don't seem concerned about this smell of smoke."

9

"I'm more concerned about the smokescreen you're putting around these Mary opportunities."

He shook his head. "You're becoming paranoid about this; there are no 'Mary opportunities'."

"No? Convenient wasn't it though, her husband being away at the time of the party?"

"You'll only believe what you want to." He sniffed. "That smell seems to have gone now."

"Good, can you get back into bed and put the light off. It's midnight and I have to get up early tomorrow. We'll continue this discussion another time"

"There's nothing else to discuss. Good night." He stretched to kiss her.

She turned her head at the last minute and brushed her lips on his cheek. "Good night. Sweet dreams … of Mary."

"Look, can we get this clear once and for all. There is nothing going on between Mary and I."

"Mary and me"

"Whatever. Nothing's going on. I love you."

"Lots of coincidences though. You know what they say, 'there's no smoke without fire'."

"And that's why I'm still going to check downstairs." He rested his hand on the door handle. "Ouch."

"I've just realised what you said. When you spoke about Mary's experience with the smoke detector you said, 'I found the flashing light in the bedroom particularly irritating' not 'I would find'."

He opened the door, and the flames found the vent they had been seeking and roared into the bedroom.

Taken for a ride

S he had the I'm-not-threatening, cheery smile, but didn't look like the usual hitch-hiker. For a start the 'uniform' was missing: no all-weather anorak and heavy walking-boots, and the obligatory doesn't-fit-in-the-boot-has-to-go-on-the-back-seat, overloaded rucksack was not propping up the wall beside her. Her close-fitting coat looked expensive and a brightly coloured scarf was wrapped around her neck against the icy wind. Black, leather, high boots completed the ensemble, and she was holding what looked like a new holdall.

Why I chose that particular motorway service station to stop at I don't know. It could have been any one of four that I use when coming back from down south, which is only two or three times a year. I like to vary it a bit. And ten o'clock was too early for my elevenses, but the car needed petrol and I was feeling a bit hung over from the sales meeting dinner the night before. I parked in the corner furthest away from the building, just in case anything should happen.

She was standing at the bottom of the steps to the restaurant. Her handwritten sign with the word 'Luton' flapped in the wind. I half-returned her smile and walked past her. At the top of the steps I turned and saw she was talking to two middle-aged ladies. She shook her head and the ladies set off to search for their car. An extra strong gust swept the car park uncoiling the flimsy material around her neck. In trying to hang on to the wayward scarf she dropped the holdall and let go of the sign, which flew away like a demented, paper aeroplane.

"Would you like a cup of coffee?"

She jumped when I spoke, and turning around she had to move back to look at me because I was two steps above her.

I felt I was being scrutinised before she spoke, then the smile returned, "Yes, OK, looks like I'll have to make a new sign anyway."

I reached down and picked up the bag, but she grabbed it from me. I couldn't help noticing how light it was.

As usual, the inside of the restaurant was oppressively warm, but she kept her coat buttoned-up as we found a table by the window.

"I'm Frank by the way."

"Claudia," she mumbled, and continued to gaze out of the window. Sadness have settled on her face, and she absent-mindedly stirred her coffee. When I'd seen her outside I'd assumed she was quite young, too young, but now she'd removed her scarf I could see that she was most probably in her mid-twenties.

"You're on your way to Luton?"

"Yes."

"And those ladies weren't going in that direction?"

"Ladies?"

"I thought those two ladies were offering you a lift."

"They were going in that direction and yes, they were offering me a lift."

"So, why didn't you go with them?"

She turned her face in my direction, that smile was there again. "They looked boring to spend an hour or so in a car with."

"But if you want to get to Luton–"

"I'm not in a hurry. I'd rather travel with someone a bit more … a bit more exciting." Again the smile, only this time her eyes deliberately met mine.

I felt myself starting to blush, and I couldn't stop something stupid tumbling out of my mouth. "Luton's not the most exciting place in the world."

"No, but I've got friends there."

"So, just a visit to see friends?"

"Something like that."

We chatted, small talk I guess it's called: the weather, the price of drinks in motorway service stations, the weather. I offered her a second coffee, but she refused. Looking back, I realise now that I didn't find out anything about her, despite asking: she cleverly sidestepped any question about herself. Once or twice her foot brushed my leg under the table as she shifted in her chair.

After a short period of silence, we spoke at the same time.

"Which direction are you–"

"I'm going in the–"

"You first," she said

"I was going to say, I'm going in the direction of Luton, but not actually to Luton, if that would help."

"My mother told me not to accept lifts from strange men." Once again her foot touched my leg.

"I'm a stranger, not a strange man, and I'm not in the habit of offering lifts to young ladies."

She scrutinised me again, smiled and said, "OK, let's go."

For the first time in my life I left a motorway service station restaurant without returning my tray to the rack. I felt guilty rushing out.

The wind was still blowing across the car park. "Where's your car?" she asked.

"Just over there." I said, pointing vaguely.

13

"Shall I wait here while you go and get it?"

"No, it's not far."

As we reached the far corner, she shouted above the wind, "I thought you said it wasn't far."

I unlocked the passenger door and waited for her to sit and swivel her legs in. She made a point of keeping her coat wrapped around her legs.

I started the engine, which still had enough residual heat to produce a stream of just warm air.

"I hope it's going to get much hotter in here," she said smiling and looking me directly in the eyes as she unbuttoned her coat. The boots stopped below the knee and then there was nothing but leg covered by black hosiery until a white skirt at the limit of decency.

I've said all along that I don't remember what happened next, or do I just want to forget. Whichever it is, it's just a blur. The piercing scream is what still echoes in my head. The sight of torn hose and ripped blouse flashes before my eyes. I remember people surrounding the car and banging on the windows Then I was being dragged out and held by two men who seemed twice as big as me. From the size of the bruise, one of them certainly kneed the back of my legs. Finally, I remember thinking I'd been rescued by the arrival of the service station security and the police.

The next time I saw Claudia was at the trial, but I hardly recognised her. She looked like a nun out of uniform: hair pulled tight in a ponytail, no makeup, and clothes that gave no hint of a body underneath. The story she told sounded like a planned assault; enticement into the restaurant, making suggestive comments, forcing her into the car (how was never explained), and trying to rape her. My story, the one written here, sounded weak even to me, and at best foolish. Several customers in the restaurant said they had seen this older man rushing out of the restaurant after a younger girl.

The jury took less than an hour to reach a guilty verdict. The judge said rape was the most despicable of crimes, and to commit an offence like this in a public car park, in daylight, showed no regard for the victim, the law or anyone else. He handed down the maximum sentence of five years.

I've been here for eighteen months now. There's only one good thing about prison, you have lots of time to think, mostly too much time. I've gone over in my mind again and again what happened that day, and I'm sure I'm innocent of the charge of rape. It didn't happen, I know it didn't. However, I'd resigned myself to having to serve my full sentence, with time off for good behaviour.

But now perhaps there's chance to have the verdict changed. A local newspaper was doing an article about the long-term psychological effects on crime victims. They interviewed Claudia. The lady reporter came to the conclusion that Claudia hated men. Nothing surprising there, but the article subtly suggested that this had not started with the attempted rape. Investigation had revealed that a few weeks before that windy day at the motorway service station, what had seemed a perfect marriage had ended when Claudia's husband ran off with his secretary. My solicitor thinks if that had been known by the jury at my trial, there would have been sufficient grounds to question if she had planned what happened as a revenge on men.

That's mainly why I've written this down, to get my story straight. I need to find a way to show how she enticed me not me her. That smile played a big part in it, but how do you describe a smile? I'll have to try to remember some of the things she said when we were drinking coffee. Together with the newspaper article that should be enough to put doubt into people's minds, at least make it my word against hers.

There's only one possible problem, small chance, but nonetheless possible. This might create a lot of local publicity. I have to hope Jessica, Maureen and Pamela don't read the newspapers too closely, and put two and two together. I don't think they'd do anything now anyway. Jessica must have been five years ago, the other two more recently, but still a couple of years have passed. None of them cried rape and they'd no reason to. After all, it was only a few fumblings in a motorway service station car park in return for promising to give them a lift.

Cramping his style

"Gerald Percival Smythe-Chambers you are charged with driving in excess of the speed limit, in-as-much-as on 24 February you were driving at 60 miles per hour in Brampton Road, where the speed limit is 30 miles per hour. How do you plead, guilty or not guilty?"

"Not guilty."

His Honour Judge Anthony Hessledon QC shook his head slightly, and moved his rimless glasses halfway down his nose. "Mr Charlton."

"If it please the court. The fact in this case is very clear. A permanent speed camera photographed Mr Smythe-Chambers' car travelling at sixty miles per hour. We enter into evidence Exhibit 1, the photographic image duly annotated with the speed and date. There's really nothing more to add." The prosecutor sat down wearily. He'd been allocated all these … one could hardly call them cases, because he only had three months left before he could dedicate all his time to his precious garden.

"Thank you Mr Charlton. Mr … " Judge Hessledon shuffled his papers. He'd not seen the defence lawyer before, and his memory was not what it used to be. "Mr Fowler, I presume your client wishes to make a statement?"

"He does Your Honour."

"Proceed."

The clerk of the court administered the oath. He backed away while Smythe-Chambers was reading it, and held his breath to retrieve the bible and card: the aftershave, probably very expensive, was overpowering.

Gerald Smythe-Chambers fixed his eyes on the judge, with his head slightly tilted to one side and his jaw sticking out.

"Mr Smythe-Chambers were you in your car on the 24 February at five-fifteen driving along Brompton Road?"

"I was."

"And were you driving at sixty miles per hour?"

Smythe-Chambers paused, keeping his eyes on the judge. "The car was travelling at sixty miles per hour, as the photograph shows, but that was not my fault."

Judge Hessledon looked up from his papers with an expression that said 'this is going to be good'.

"Explain please Mr Smythe-Chambers."

"I had cramp in my right leg and could not move it from the accelerator."

"So, when the car passed the speed camera, the car was essentially out of your control?"

"Yes."

"Thank you Mr Smythe-Chambers."

"That's it Mr Fowler?"

"Yes, Your Honour, The car was travelling at sixty miles per hour, but because of the cramp Mr Smythe-Chambers was not guilty of driving at sixty miles per hour."

Again a shake of the head from Judge Hessledon. "I'm sure you have some questions Mr Charlton."

"I do indeed, Your Honour. So, Mr Smythe-Chambers, if I understand correctly, your claim is that your foot was stuck on the accelerator making the car travel at twice the speed limit."

18

Smythe-Chambers' eyes remained fixed on the judge, who was now studying him intently. "That's correct."

"Tell me Mr Smythe-Chambers, do you often get these attacks of cramp?"

"No, not often."

"But you did on this occasion?"

"Yes."

"But of course there's no evidence that you did."

"My calf muscle still feels sore, but there's nothing to see. I can show you if you like." There was laughter from the public gallery as Smythe-Chambers started to reach down below the level of the witness box.

"I don't think that will be necessary, do you Mr Charlton?

"No, Your Honour."

Smythe-Chambers re-emerged. "Actually I can feel it stiffening-up a bit now."

"Well if that happens we may take a look," said the judge, and allowed the laughter from the gallery again. "Mr Charlton."

"So why do you think this sudden bout of cramp happened at this precise, unfortunate moment?"

Smythe-Chambers glanced towards Mr Fowler, who gave an almost imperceptible nod.

"It's a long story."

"The court wants to hear, Mr Smythe-Chambers, take your time."

Smythe-Chambers now gave the judge the full intensity of his stare. "It all began when I lost the stick that contained all my information. I–"

The judge looked over the top of his glasses, which had now reached the end of his nose. "Did you say 'stick' Mr Smythe-Chambers? What type of stick?"

19

Mr Fowler, who was handling his first case in court and was eager, almost overeager to impress, jumped to his feet "If it please the court I–"

"No, it does not Mr Fowler, let your client explain.

Smythe-Chambers' expression became one of 'doesn't everyone know?' contempt, which the judge recognised and ignored as only a judge can. "A stick is a flash memory card for a computer."

The prosecutor and the judge looked at each another.

"I'd only recently decided to buy a two-giga stick so that–"

The judge cleared his throat. "I'm sorry to interrupt again Mr Smythe-Chambers, but 'two-giga' did you say?"

There was the start of laughter from the gallery, which the judge silenced by raising his gavel, but not letting it fall.

"Two Gigabyte."

"A byte is a measure of memory capacity, Your Honour. Giga means a thousand million bytes."

"Thank you Mr Fowler, I think that makes everything clear. Mr Charlton?"

The prosecutor inclined his head. A gesture the judge was not hoping for; it certainly was not clear to him, and he doubted to the prosecutor either. "Continue Mr Smythe-Chambers."

"So with this two-giga stick I could archive all the files from my laptop. Losing the stick should have been no problem, of course, because the files were still on my hard disk." Smythe-Chambers looked from judge to, prosecutor. They guessed, rightly, that this was a place to nod their agreement. "So you can imagine my absolute horror that night when I switched on my computer and it wouldn't boot properly." Again he looked for sympathy, and got it, although they seemed even less sure this time. "So I'd lost everything. Everything."

This time the two people he was addressing decided shaking the head was more appropriate.

The prosecutor rose. "Your Honour, do we really need to hear all this? Is all this relevant?"

"Mr Fowler is all this relevant."

"Yes, Your Honour, and I think you will see why in just a minute."

"I hope it's not much longer than a minute."

"No, Your Honour."

"Carry on Mr Smythe-Chambers."

"I tried running the recovery CD and a disk repair, but neither worked. Catastrophe!"

The judge and the prosecutor had given up pretending to understand and just stared blankly at Smythe-Chambers.

He took that to mean they understood.

"Of course, now I had no pop-up reminders of important dates. I was lost, completely lost, you can imagine."

The prosecutor was on his way up again, but the judge waved him down.

"Mr Smythe-Chambers could you get to the point of the speeding incident."

"Yes, Your Honour, sorry Your Honour. I just wanted you to understand the devastation I felt. So, with no pop-ups, two days later I forgot my girlfriend's birthday, or almost forgot. Fortunately at half past four a friend of mine called me and asked if I'd be going to the squash club that night, or was I taking Fiona, that's my girlfriend, out to dinner for her birthday. Panic. Absolute panic. I told my secretary to book a restaurant and I dashed off to buy some flowers. I was feeling really nervous. I guess it was this situation coming on top of all the trauma with my laptop. When I get nervous I start stretching my fingers." He demonstrated with his hands on the edge of the witness box. "and toes. As I was driving I continued to do this, I couldn't help it. As you know, if you continue to do this the muscle can become fatigued because it doesn't relax, resulting in a sustained contraction of the muscle, what we call 'cramp'. And that's what happened in my right leg. I couldn't get it off the accelerator and my speed just went up and up. Fortunately there were no other cars around. I eventually used my left foot on the brake and forced my right foot off the accelerator. So, you see the speed was not my fault. It all happened because of my lost memory stick and a broken hard disk."

There was absolute silence in the court.

"Mr Charlton?"

The prosecutor looked as though he was coming out of a trance. "I have no further questions, Your Honour."

The judge looked down at his papers for two minutes, although he read nothing. "Mr Smythe-Chambers either what you told us is a very sad story or a lot of technical mumbo-jumbo, which for your information means nonsense. As I don't want to waste the court's time by hearing your story again to try to understand it, which I doubt very much I would, I'm prepared to give you the benefit of the doubt. The fact remains that you were still driving extremely fast, and, therefore, putting other people's lives in danger. However, you will not be banned from driving. You will receive three penalty points on your licence and pay a fine of one thousand pounds." This time the judge's gavel did fall.

Gerald Percival Smythe-Chambers left the court building flanked by Mr Fowler and his girlfriend. As they walked down the long flight of stairs leading to the front exit, he suddenly stumbled and fell down the last six steps.

Mr Fowler helped him to his feet. "Are you all right?"

"Yes, thank you. I must be getting old, that's the first time I've ever had cramp in my right leg."

They stared at each other with wide eyes.

My father's love

The hearse pulled away from the kerb and advanced at walking pace down the narrow street. In the 'close-family' car behind we were near enough to read the words on the card of the wreath placed at the end of the coffin - 'I love you - (signed) Ken Appleton'.

"I couldn't think of anything else to put", said my Dad between sobs.

Was he crying for her or for him? What would my Mam have said if she had seen the card? Like me, would she have thought it a sham? They had never seemed close, but perhaps the things that happened in my early years clouded my opinion. Seen through the eyes of a child, it had been a frightening relationship with deep troughs of anger, and scattered, but high peaks of happiness. But, then again, what does a child know of the love between a man and a woman?

However, even looking back from the advantage of age, I can't recall anything between them of the affection that I now associate with love. Isn't it usually the happy childhood memories that stick in the mind? Don't we try to push the bad memories so far back that they disappear from the conscious recollection process? Why then do I find it impossible to believe the words written by my Dad on the card are anything but that, 'words on a card'?

Perhaps they never had a real chance to fall in love. They'd met and married when the world was in turmoil; when not knowing for how long one would be alive made short-term pleasures and comfort more of a reason for coming together than love.

My future mother was a four-foot-eight-and-a-half searchlight operator, and my future father a six-foot paratrooper. Both came from simple backgrounds, although hers was probably slightly more up the social scale of the time. She had already been engaged to the owner of a small shop, who would've probably been able to provide a better life for her than my Dad: something she told him on more than one occasion.

I arrived after two years and my sister three years later. Surely those must have been happy times: young couple with a new family? Obviously my personal memory doesn't stretch back that far. I only know that one of my earliest recollections, at what age I don't know, was having to sit with an aunt in the corridor of some building that had the smell of dust and old furniture polish. My Mam and Dad had an appointment. They were 'going to court to talk to a judge', and I might have to talk to the judge. The meaning and significance of this was lost on me at the time.

It seems not long after this, but it could have been months or years, there was the policeman incident. I remember my Mam throwing a cup of tea in my Dad's face. The tea was cold and for some reason my Dad had his overcoat on, so there was no real damage. I knew my Mam could not stand the taste of tea, but even at whatever age I was, I thought this was a strange thing to do. My Dad went out and came back with a policeman. What I don't recall is my Dad getting angry, perhaps that was a sign of love.

But these memories are like old films that have run through the projector so many times they start to lose some of the sharpness of their image, and the endings are missing. Much more vivid is the absence of a picture of my Dad during my first five years in school. He'd volunteered to rejoin the army, and was in Japan. Perhaps it would have been better if they had divorced: at least my Mam, sister and I would not have spent so much time wondering when he was coming home.

My Mam seemed to swing between deep depression and light-hearted, girlish joy. I was too young to even consider thinking about what caused these sometimes dramatic mood changes. I just learned what to do; keep out of her way or look forward to a special treat. I thought sometimes she took out her anger at my Dad on me, but maybe that was just my childish imagination. Always after being angry with me she would tell me I was special to her, and she was glad I would never grow up to be like him.

The return of my Dad on leave, usually unexpectedly, always had a strange effect on my Mam. She seemed to be pleased and disappointed at the same time. A short time after he arrived back, my Mam usually became ill and my Dad had to take her upstairs to bed. She must have fainted, which she was prone to do. I could hear the bed springs bouncing up and down, presumably my Dad trying to revive her, and my Mam moaning.

They were very happy for the few days he was there, and we all missed him when it came time for him to leave. My Mam even had one of her fainting spells just before he left.

When my Dad came home for good, we looked like a normal family. The kids went to school, the Father went to work, and the Mother stayed at home and cooked and cleaned. We went to the park when the sun shone and huddled round the fire and the wireless on wet winter nights. On some Saturday nights my parents went out, leaving me to babysit my sister. 'Out' for them meant the pictures or the pub with friends. They usually returned in a good mood.

25

The dark side came when they argued, which they did often. I don't know what about. My sister and I were rarely there when it started. But we knew something was wrong from the volume of silence which filled the house. Silence that is, from my Dad. My Mam ranted and raved, but he just sat with an expressionless face. Then, and even more so now, I wonder why he didn't say anything. Perhaps I should ask him one day.

Some years after I left home, my Dad had what my Mam referred to as an 'affair'. Bestowing such a title on what happened gave it an air of sophistication that it certainly did not have. True, there was another woman; someone my Dad worked with. But if anything more happened than a few quick fumbles, I'd be surprised. My Mam told me she realised that she had probably driven my Dad to it; he said it was not something he had wanted to do. My telling them both to come to their senses seemed to work.

I'd moved to another country by this stage, and I did not see much of them. During my visits at least it seemed that in the early winter of their lives they had reached a tranquil understanding of each other, or was it just a resigned tolerance? Arguments, yes, but without the ferocity on my Mam's side, and the silences got shorter, as if they both realised time was running out.

The funeral was a week ago. Dad has not said anything except, "Yes, please", " No, thank you", or "I don't mind". At least I've persuaded him to come out to the pub. The silence continues through half of his pint of bitter.

"Do you remember Ken?"

"Sorry Dad, what did you say?"

"Do you remember Ken?"

"Ken? Ken who?"

"Ken who had the shop."

"Ken? Shop? I'm afraid I don't know what you're talking about, Dad"

"Ken, with the shop on the bridge, in town. You met him. Probably many times, with your Mam."

"Ah, that Ken. Yes, I vaguely remember him. What about him?"

"You knew that he and your Mam were ... were ..."

"Weren't they engaged before you and Mam met?"

"Not 'before', actually at the time."

"And you came along and swept her off her feet, eh"

By the expression on his face, my attempt at humour hasn't worked.

"They continued to see each other."

"I'm sure that's not true."

"Oh it is. I was still on active war service."

This conversation will only make him more depressed.

"Well, that's all in the past now."

Silence.

"You should have been told,"

"Told what?"

"He was your father."

"What? What are you saying?"

"Your Mam couldn't give him up. When I came back, she was pregnant."

"But ... why ... did ... why did you stay together?"

"I told her it didn't matter, that I understood. Those were uncertain times. It happened a lot. And we were married."

"So, you ... you pretended that I belonged to both of you."

"It didn't seem like pretending. I thought of you as mine."

I want to put my arms around him, but it will embarrass him if I do.

Silence.

"But, when you came back, that was the end of their relationship, right Dad?"

27

"What makes you ask that?"

"Something ... something that struck me at the time as being a bit odd, but I didn't want to say anything."

"What?"

"The wreath from you, it was signed 'Ken Appleton'. Why not just 'Ken'?"

"I wanted her to know it was from me, and not from him, Ken Marsden"

"Could she have thought that? Were they still in contact?"

"As far as I know, until last year."

"But all that time? Why? Why did you let it go on?"

"Because I loved her."

One day

C hristopher was pleased to get his glasses. Screwing up his eyes to read had become automatic for him. When the teacher in the second year at school had asked him why, he'd simply answered, "I always do, Miss". But the glasses started the problems.

"Where's yer girlfriend four-eyes?"

Christopher always managed to find a quiet spot on the far side of the playground where he could eat his playtime snack in peace. But on the first day at school with the glasses the Fletcher gang, Brian Fletcher, the Adams twins, and little Billy Evans, spotted him and surrounded him.

Brian Fletcher stood directly in front of him. "Doesn't Margo like yer goggles?"

"She's not my girlfriend."

"We saw yer kissing her."

"Kiss, kiss, kiss" chanted the gang.

"I didn't kiss her." Under his breath Christopher said, "I'm sorry Jesus for this lie".

"What yer got in yer box?"

Christopher hugged the Tupperware closer to his chest.

"Come on goggle-eyes, I wanna to see what yer eating."

Brian grabbed the box, but Christopher hung on. When he realised he wouldn't get it, Brian gave the box a heavy shove.

Billy Evans had knelt down behind Christopher, sending him falling backwards. As he put his hands behind him to break the fall, the Tupperware box flew up and Brian caught it. Christopher's glasses slipped down his nose and on to the ground. Brian struggled to open the box.

"What's going on here?

"Nothing Miss."

"You're not bullying people again are you Brian Fletcher?"

"No Miss."

Miss Plummer lifted Christopher to his feet and retrieved his undamaged glasses. "Are you OK?"

"Yes, Miss Plummer."

""Yes, Miss Plummer""

"Do you say something Fletcher?"

"No Miss Plummer."

"Good. Now go and get on with your break, you've only got a few more minutes."

Brian's gang galloped away on their imaginary horses.

"You don't want to let them bully you, Christopher."

"No. Miss."

But both knew it wouldn't be the last time.

As long as he was in the infants it was only playtime he had to worry about because his mum came to meet him at lunchtime and the end of the day. She continued to do this when he moved to the juniors, but Christopher asked her to stop. "I'm a big boy now Mum, it's embarrassing when you're waiting for me." This was a mistake, because now he was the target three times a day. At least at lunchtime and the end of the day he could rush out and run home to escape.

Chocolate and sweets became comforters to compensate for the tormenting. As he grew in height, he also increased in width.

"Oi, fatso, 'ave yer brought a big towel with yer today?" Billy Evans knew that, at the other side of the changing room, he was at a safe distance in the unlikely event that Christopher reacted to his words.

Tom Adams joined in "Or are yer going outside to roll in the mud to dry yerself, like other hippopotamuses?

"Hippo, hippo, hippo," rang out the chorus.

Fletcher, muscular for a ten-year-old from the boxing training he did, strolled over to Christopher, and the chanting stopped. "How come yer let in three goals today, Fatso? We put yer in goal because you almost fill it, and then yer let in three."

"Sorry Fletch, the mud splashed my glasses, and I couldn't see properly."

"I'm Fletcher to you four-eyes. Is that clear?" He pushed his face close to Christopher.

"Yes, Fletcher."

"Good. What d'yer think, should I punch him for letting in three goals?"

"Punch, punch, punch."

"Evans, watch out for PT Smith." Fletcher took up a boxing stance, the crowd cheered, and Christopher cowered.

Fletcher relaxed. "Nah, I'd be afraid to lose me'and in all that fat."

During all this Harry Adams had sneaked up behind Christopher, and with one swift action whipped the towel from around his waist, to great cheers.

You wait, thought Christopher, one day …

Christopher was only one of three people in his year who passed the exams for the grammar school. Without the help of the credit cards his parents wouldn't have been able to afford the uniform and all the accessories that went with it.

"Well, well, look who's here, it's Christopher the swot."

The Adams twins and little Billy Evans danced round him. "Swot, swot, swot."

"Get out of my way, Fletcher."

"And what if I don't?"

"Swot, swot, swot."

"I have to get home."

"Got to do yer homework have yer?"

"Homework's for puffs," shouted Billy, backing away out of reach, just in case.

"Yeah, puffs." Added one of the Adams twins, although Christopher was never sure which one was which.

"Puff, puff, puff."

Christopher took a step towards Billy, and Fletcher immediately moved in front of him.

"Hit him Fletch." Billy peeked round the side of Fletcher.

"Nah, he'll only run and tell his mummy."

"Mummy's boy, mummy's boy, mummy's boy."

"You're all jealous because I'm at grammar school and you're not."

"Jealous? I wouldn't want to go to that puffy school, especially when they make you wear this crap uniform."

Fletcher shaped-up to hit Christopher, but instead made a grab for his cap. Not for the first time Christopher just stood and watched as his blue and gold-hooped cap was flung between the four youths. They quickly tired of their game, and Fletcher held the cap over a puddle.

"Let's see how fast you are swot."

Christopher tried, but he knew he was too far away.

The four ran off. "Swot, swot, swot."

"What happened to your cap again?"

"I'm sorry Mum, it fell off."

"I can never understand how a cap can fall off your head. You should be more careful. Your uniform costs a lot of money. I go out to work at night to pay for that. Do you appreciate it? No. I work my fingers to the bone and you can't even keep you cap on your head. We're not made of money you know. Not like the parents of some of those rich kids you mix with now at grammar school. I wish we hadn't sent you. I've said before, you'll only become stuck-up and we won't be good enough for you."

"Sorry."

"One day you'll be sorry," said his mother.

Those louts who dropped my cap in the water will be sorry, thought Christopher, one day.

Christopher graduated top of his class at the police training school. He would have chosen not to be stationed in the district where he was born and brought up, but the old sergeant told him, "It's better for you lad. You've got a lot to learn and it helps if you're more familiar with the territory".

In his second week the station got a 999 call reporting a burglary in progress. They caught the thieves in the act.

The custody officer asked, "Who is the arresting officer?"

"I am," said Christopher. "Brian Fletcher, Tom Adams, Harry Adams, and Billy Evans I'm arresting you for unlawfully breaking and entering 43 Windslow Road. You are not obliged to say anything, but anything you do say may be taken down and used in evidence against you." Christopher could not help a small smile creasing the corners of his mouth, and a barely audible word escaping "Today."

The last cuckoo

"Cuck... cuck..."
What's happening?
"Cuck... cuck..."
Ah! I can't cuckoo.
The door's not opening
Don't panic.
Try again.
"Cuc... Cuc..."
Even worse!
It was all right fifteen minutes ago.
Don't say that young trainee forgot to wind me. Pretty little thing she is, but I'm not so sure all her cogs mesh. Yes, she did, I'm sure. I remember feeling flushed when she pulled my chain! Flushed ... chain ... get it? But did she give me a real 24-hour wind by pulling it all the way down?
"Cuc... Cuc..."
Too late now. Stop trying. Even if it works now, it looks stupid doing it after the moment has passed.
Tick, tock, tick ... 4, 5, 6 ...
See what happens in fifteen minutes.
It wasn't like this in the old days. There was never any question of being neglected. That was of course before they came along - the quartzes. With their, 'we don't need any

attention, we run continuously, and we're accurate to within one second in 50 years'. 50 years - pff! If they last that long.

"And what happens when your battery needs changing?" I told them. Of course, they had no answer to that.

Look at me. I mean, I'm a work of precision engineering, built by a craftsman, someone who trained for years under the watchful (punny!) eye of the aged artisan. There's generations of skills in me. Skills that have been handed down through the years. I'm part of the Swiss heritage of attention to detail that started in the cottages of the poor, but proud peasants high in the Alps.

Well, that's not 100% true. In fact, it's not even 50% right or even 10%. It's completely untrue. I came from a factory in North London. Put together by a redundant dockworker following a colour-coded plan. But they don't know that. At least the factory was owned by someone who lives in Swiss Cottage.

Tick, tock, tick ... 55, 56, 57...

Stand-by to move the minute hand on a notch. Opps! There we go.

Tick, tock, tick ... 1, 2, 3 ...

I may come from a factory, but at least I've got some style. What do these quartz types know? I mean, look at them. Some of them have no moving parts, just numbers that stare at you. What's that got to do with time? I ask you. Time's something you need hands to display. Hands that point. Everyone knows that when my big hand is at six and the little hand at eleven it's time to think about lunch. Who needs to know that it's eleven thirty-two?

Some of them have hands of course. They had to do that when they saw that people had got over the fad of illuminated numbers. Some even tick - completely artificially of course.

Speaking of ticking, how are we doing?

Tick, tock, tick ... 32, 33, 34 ...

OK for the moment, nothing to do for a while.

How long have I been here now? Must be months. Why haven't I been sold? When I see some of the things people buy ... it's amazing.

Look at her over there for example. No, not the bright blue creation with big numbers; that's strictly for the kitchen. Although why anyone would want it even there, I can't imagine. No, the one, with the glass dome. Look at the size of the face, can you read it? It's so small, and those Roman numerals all bunched up together, impossible. And, as for those revolving brass balls ... all show. But four of those were sold last week. It's beyond me.

Tick, tock, tick ... 58, 59, 60

Minute hand moved, geared through to hour hand, moved on a fraction. Is that too much? No, looks OK.

Soon be time to try the cuckoo again. I hope it works this time. The others are going to think it very funny if they don't hear me. Many of them rely on me to regulate themselves. Mind you, those who are always complaining about what they call the 'din' every quarter of an hour will probably be pleased.

Let's just have a quick check. Pendulum swinging - yes; bird connected to minute hand lever - yes; sound generator plunger ready - yes. Seems to be all in order.

Tick, tock, tick ... 58, 59, 60.

"Ookcuc, ookcuc..."

What!

"Ookcuc, ookcuc..."

Stop this. People are staring. Good thing the bird didn't get out of the door.

This is serious.

I bet it's something to do with that oil the apprentice put on my main drive wheel yesterday. I thought he didn't know what he was doing - pointing the oilcan in a general direction inside me and squirting. And, I didn't like the smell of that oil too much. It was even worse than the gunge they used in the factory.

Maybe I can get someone to help me. Let me see, who haven't I upset recently?

There's big Grandfather down there. He's probably in the best position to give me a check over, but his eyesight is not too good, and he's almost certainly in one of his grumpy moods. He looks asleep. He'll wake up on the hour when his gong goes off. Nobody can sleep through that!

The Swatches are always friendly, I think. I can't understand a word they're saying actually. When they first arrived, they obviously thought I was also Swiss and started babbling away, 'Grützi, gahts?' I just ignored them: stupid foreigners. They wouldn't be any help in any case, too busy admiring each other's fancy straps and faces.

Tick, tock, tick ... 26, 27, 28 ...

Everything else seems to be working OK, except for the cuckoo sound.

What about the pretty little Copper Alarm that came in the other day? Might be a way to get to know her; I'd like to ring her bell. But if there were something wrong with me, I wouldn't want her to see me not at my best. Anyway, she seems to taken up with that Electronic Waker-up, the one with the green digits and snooze control; best of luck to them; it'll never work.

I could ask one of the upmarket types. I haven't upset them recently. In fact not at all. I never have any contact with them. They wouldn't lower themselves to talk to me I suppose. Who do they think they are? Just because they've got names like Rolex and Patek Philippe, doesn't mean to say they're any better than me. Diamonds, gold, platinum, what difference do they make? "We all measure time, mate"

What am I going to do?

Tick, tock, tick ... 42, 43, 44 ...

Look, I've got to do something, the situation is getting desperate.

I know. What about that old Hallstand piece? Yes, he owes me a favour. When he had trouble with striking the hour a few weeks ago, I distracted attention away from him and got him out of trouble by giving an extra loud "Cuckoo", which is what I wish I could do now. Yes, he'll help me. Everyone says he's a 'chiming' fellow - oh, is there no end to my wit, even under these circumstances?

"Psst, psst, Hallstand."

"Who me?"

"Yes, you Sir" You old fool. "Do you think you could do me a small favour?", better talk to him in his style, or he'll pretend to not understand me.

"If I can."

"Can you see all of me from where you are?"

"Yes, just about."

"Well, just check out my chains, there's a good fellow. Make sure nothing is tangled."

"I can't see any problems."

"Are you sure?" Probably as blind as a bat

"Sure. Everything looks in order."

"Thanks mate."

So, that's not the problem.

Tick, tock, tick ... 35, 36, 37 ...

Coming up to the hour. 8 am. An important point for me. If I can't do this, then something is really wrong. Not that anyone else will notice at this time. Everyone is too busy making sure that everything is synchronised for the start of the next 60 minutes.

I'm going to make a really big effort.

Tick, tock, tick ... 55, 56, 57 ...

Are we ready? Deep breath.

"Cuckoo ..."

Ah, what a relief, everything seems to be OK.

"Cuckoo, Cuckooooooooooooooooooooo ..."

Stop!

"...oooooooooooooo..."

Now is the time to panic

"...oooooooooooooo..."

What can I do? There's nothing in my mechanism that allows for this to happen.

"...oooooooooooooo..."

The others are beginning to notice, now that they have finished their hourly tasks.

"Do be quiet cuckoo and stop showing off."

"I would if I could, Grandfather. I would if I could."

"...oooooooooooooo..."

"Shiver me timbers, matey, you sound like a force nine."

"I know, Ship's, I know."

"...oooooooooooooo..."

"Höre auf!"

"I'm trying, Swissy, believe me, I'm trying."

"...oooooooooooooo..."

"WHAT CAN I DO?"

"...oooooooooooooo... cuckooooooooooooooooooooooo... "

"Prease honourable cuckoo sah, prease to be quiet."

"But what can I do, Orient?"

"Honourabe fing, to commit hara-kiri."

"What, you mean? ... No!"

"...oooooooooooooo..."

"Ony fing to do."

"But ... but"

He's right, I suppose. Slip the cogs until the pendulum rests on the floor. What a way to go!

"Goodbye cruel world. The time has come for me to clock out."

"...ooooooooooooooooooooooo."

"............................"

"............................"

"Good morning Mr Mainspring"

"Good morning Miss Bell. Time to open up the shop."

"That Swiss cuckoo clock seems to have stopped, Mr Mainspring. Shall I wind it up?"

"No. I've already tried. It's broken. I thought it sounded funny yesterday. The problem with those cheaper models is that you can't get the parts to repair them. I guess we'll have to throw it away."

"CUC!"

Welcome to the avenue

The woman over the road is painting her front door green. I just happen to be standing at the window in my front bedroom scanning the Avenue through my binoculars, part of my neighbourhood watch duties, and there she is, bold as brass, painting away at eight thirty in the morning. Why, I ask myself? What is she doing? And green of all colours. What was wrong with the previous colour? All our front doors are brown or dark-blue. Green's going to lower the tone of the Avenue.

They only moved in a few weeks ago. What are they doing painting the front door already, before they've had a chance to get to know the area? They should have waited until after they've been invited to the Residents Association.

I've heard some things about her. Not that I listen to or spread rumours of course, not like some people around here. But her next door neighbour, Mrs Watkins-Ralston, was talking to Mrs Chapwin from number 26 the other day in the fresh-farm-produce greengrocer's; they have such high-quality products there. I just happened to overhear her say that there'd been some strange noises coming from that house. Mrs Chapwin asked her what she meant by 'strange noises', and Mrs Watkins-Ralston said it sounded like someone banging a tambourine. Perhaps they are members of the

Salvation Army. I do hope not: all those tramps and dirty people.

I'm a light sleeper and sometimes I've woken up at six in the morning and just happened to look out of the window. I've seen him going out. What type of job does he have? He doesn't carry a briefcase. I mean, that can't be right, can it, going out in the middle of the night. It is certainly not the sort of thing we are used to in the Avenue.

And now the wife of the new owner of the Mulfort's house is painting the front door green. I must speak to Mrs Watkins-Ralston, but I'll wait half an hour until the respectable time of nine o'clock.

"Good morning, Cynthia Parkinson here."

"Good morning Mrs Parkinson."

"I was just wondering Mrs Watkins-Ralston if you have looked out of your window this morning and observed what is happening next door?"

"I have indeed. Mr Watkins-Ralston left for his office in a most unhappy frame of mind."

"I can imagine."

"He is going to telephone Mr Chapwin and suggest a meeting of the Residents Association tonight. Will you and Mr Parkinson be able to be there?"

"We most certainly will."

Harold, my husband, and I are already seated at the Chapwin's large dining table when I see the Blackburns, the other newcomers in the Avenue, arrive. I tell Harold to move along one chair so I can sit between the Blackburns and explain who everyone is: this is their first Residents Association meeting.

"Good evening Mr Blackburn, Mrs Blackburn. I'm Mrs Parkinson"

"Please call me Bill."

"And Maggie."

I swallow and force a smile. "William and Margaret. This is my husband Mr Parkinson."

"I'd like to call this meeting to order, at … nine … thirty-two pm."

I keep my voice low and speak in the direction of Mr Blackburn. *That's Mr Chapwin, of Chapwin and Braintree, Chartered Accountants. He's the chairman of the Association.*

"Duly noted in the minutes Mr Chairman."

"Mr Watkins-Ralston, also an accountant, and, although a senior partner, not with his own business."

"I'd like to welcome Mr and Mrs Blackburn to their first Residents Association meeting." said Mr Chapwin.

"Hear, hear."

"This extraordinary meeting is to discuss the new residents in the Mulfort's house. We did not invite them tonight because I think there are some things we, as an Association, need to discuss first."

"Hear, hear."

"Who would like to start?"

"They're much too young to be able to afford a house in the Avenue."

"Mrs Watkins-Ralston, ex-matron, and next door neighbour of the new people."

"What is that car they have? It's not a make I recognise. I'd have run it through the computer if I'd still been with the force. Looks foreign"

"Chief Superintendent Baker, Metropolitan Police, retired.

"They're not English you know."

"Not English! How do you know Mrs Watkins-Ralston?"

"Mrs Chapwin, our hostess for tonight. We take it in turns. I'm looking forward to seeing the inside of your house."

"But if they're not English what are they doing in the Avenue?" I ask.

"I say, jolly interesting having someone different here, what. What do you think they are Mrs Watkins-Ralston?"

"That's Mrs Baker."

"I don't think, Mrs Baker, I know. They're Polish."

"You sound jolly sure."

"The eyes. In nursing you learn to tell a lot from people's eyes. And the postman left a package for them with me. It was addressed to Dr Wondsinski. That's Polish isn't it?"

"Knew some Polish chaps during the war."

"Colonel Langford, Coldstream Guards, retired, widower, usually goes to sleep at these meetings, has a heart condition."

"Fine fellows, a bit shifty, but fine fellows."

"If he's Polish, he's probably a plumber." Mr Blackburn starts to laugh, but no one else sees his joke.

Mr Watkins-Ralston looks up from his minutes. "Did you say you spoke to him, my dear?"

"No, I didn't want to make first contact like that. I left the parcel on the doorstep just before the time I knew he usually arrives home."

"Did you say Dr Wondsinski?" I ask.

Mrs Watkins-Ralton's look says 'weren't you listening'. "That's what it said on the parcel."

"Do you think he's a medical doctor?"

"Mrs Thomas, wife of the headmaster of the local school. I think that's the first thing she's said at one of these meetings."

"Doesn't look like a doctor and as matron I've worked with a few."

"Poland's always been like Italy, anybody who's been near a university is called 'doctor'."

"My husband knows about these things, he's professor of history of the Outer Hebrides at the University. He appeared on Mastermind once, but got some very unfair questions."

44

"I wonder if she's Polish also. She looks very gypsyish to me."

I wouldn't have expected Mrs Blackburn to speak at her first meeting. I don't think she should judge people by how they look.

"Could be, married to a Pole, they come across the border from Romania,"

That's Mr Thomas the headmaster."

"I didn't think Poland had a border with Romania."

Mr Thomas looked at Mr Blackburn over the top of his half-moon glasses. "Oh yes, it does. I taught geography."

"Well as long as she doesn't go round door-to-door selling clothes pegs." I say.

Mr Blackburn starts to laugh again, and then realises I am serious.

"She'd need a licence for that. I know, we used to issue them at the Met."

Mr Chapwin rises. "The question is what are we going to do about them. This painting the front door green is, in my opinion, only the start of a whole lot of trouble."

There are nods around the table, and individual conversations break out. Mr Chapwin moves round behind the people seated pouring wine from the Waterford-crystal decanter. Mrs Chapwin encourages people to help themselves to the delicate little sandwiches she always prepares. They are nice, but everyone prefers my canapés and vol-au-vents.

"I move that we send a delegation from this Association to talk to this Walondsanski fellow."

"Thank you Colonel Langford."

"I agree,"

"Me too."

"But what will you say to him?"

There are looks of surprise, if not shock, around the table. Mr Blackburn has only spoken three times and two of those have questioned what someone has said.

"As Chairman of the Residents Association I will point out to him that we have certain standards here in the Avenue, and green front doors do not fit in with those standards."

"Hear, hear."

"Nobody gave us a set of rules when we arrived."

"You are different Mr Blackburn, you are not a foreigner."

"I'm from the north of England."

"Yes, indeed, but you still wouldn't paint your front door green."

"Now it's funny you should say that, because I was thinking only the other day ..." He winces as his wife's elbow crashes with his arm.

"So, all those in favour of the Colonel's motion, please raise your hands." Mr Chapwin looks around the table. "Those against? Abstentions? Let the minutes show that the motion was carried with only Mr Blackburn against, and Mrs Blackburn abstaining."

"After you Mrs Parkinson."

"Thank you Colonel." I lead the way up the path to the green door. I am not totally comfortable with being part of the delegation, but it was decided there should be one lady accompanying Mr Chapwin and the Colonel. Mrs Watkins-Ralston put herself forward, of course, but as she is the next door neighbour, and perhaps too close to the situation, I was asked to take on the role. I couldn't have imagined any of the other ladies volunteering in any case.

We've almost reached that horrible door when the Colonel suddenly clutches his chest and falls to the floor.

I scream.

Mr Chapwin freezes.

The green door opens and a man rushes out. He bends down beside the Colonel and starts pushing on his chest. He continues this until the ambulance arrives.

"On behalf of the Association I'd like to extend a warm welcome to Dr and Mrs Wondsinski to this meeting. I know I speak for all the residents of the Avenue when I say how much we appreciate what you did for Colonel Langford. Without your swift action he would have almost certainly died."

"We agreed at our last meeting that we thought you were both going to be very welcome additions to the Avenue. We are impressed by the way you had already quickly taken steps to brighten up the Mulfort's dull house by painting the front door green. Our little delegation was on its way to convey this message to you when this unfortunate incident happened. It is some considerable comfort to us all to know we have a doctor in the Avenue."

"Thank you Mr Chafwin, but not a doctor medical, PhD architect. How you call it, CPR yes, come from army training. No job for architect in Poland. So I sell my business, learn new job and come to your country. I am plumber now."

Do you dance when you're working?

He stretched, lazily. Anjum must be making breakfast he thought, although the water lapping against the small jetty below the window meant he heard no sounds from the kitchen.

The sight of the morning mist lifting from the water was one reason he liked coming here. He always derived maximum pleasure from it by slowly sweeping the horizon. But this morning his eyes did not make the full journey. They became fixed on the lifeless figure of Anjum, hanging from a branch that oscillated under her weight. The rhythmic dipping of her feet and ankles pushed the water against the wooden posts of the jetty.

He sat and watched, nodding his head in time to the pulses on the water. His fist hit the bed as tears formed. Love and hate in equal quantities collided on his face and neutralised each other.

Just when they thought it was all in the past.

"It will be like any couple having a holiday," Anjum had said.

They stood on the left of the three-sided bar, far enough away from the dance floor to avoid the resonant effects of the base beat from the speakers, but near enough to keep an eye on the gyrating female bodies. Amsterdam's Friday night party people were out in force. Most were local, but some came from the five-star hotel above.

Paul and Berry had started the evening as usual when their business took them to Amsterdam, at The Sherry Bar. It too had been crowded, but they'd managed to find a place on the ground floor where the regulars went. They'd eaten at the little restaurant two doors along the canal, and now they were having a beer in one of their favourite late-evening places. If nothing was happening here, they'd move on.

Berry saw her first, but Paul was the one who couldn't take his eyes off her.

She was standing against the bar, gently nodding her head to the beat of the music. Her deeply tanned face and the bright redness of her lips captivated Paul. Her long, black, tightly curled hair had a shininess that made it glisten in the sweeping spotlights. To say that bells rang and fireworks went off would be melodramatic, but something happened.

"Shall we have another one here?" said Berry.

"Yes. I think we might be staying for a while."

"Fallen in love again, have you?"

"Afraid so." The flippancy of the words and the seriousness in Paul's voice did not quite match.

They drank and watched. Several men approached her, but each time she shook her head.

"What's a beautiful girl like that doing alone on a Friday night?" mused Paul.

"I wouldn't try that, it's one of the oldest lines in the book," said Berry.

"No, but it's strange, isn't it? A girl alone comes to a disco bar and then refuses to dance."

"Perhaps she prefers women."

Fifteen minutes later Paul straightened his tie, "Time to make every guy in the room jealous."

49

"No chance," said Berry.

"Good evening, would you like to dance?"

"No thank you." Her response was friendly, but left no space for discussion.

"OK ... Tell me, I'm curious; I've been watching you for some time, why don't you dance with anyone?

"Do you dance when you're working?"

"Working? Here? Doing ... Ah, I see. Really?"

"Yes, really. If you're not buying, please move on, otherwise I'll be in trouble."

"Trouble? You mean someone is watching you?"

"Yes. Now, move away. Please."

"I told you. No chance." Paul hardly noticed Berry's grin of satisfaction.

"Yes, you were right, but not for the reasons you think."

"Maybe I should go and show you how it's done."

"No. That wouldn't be a good idea. Not unless ..."

"Unless what?"

"Yes, why don't you show me how it's done?"

"Want to make a little bet?"

"No, I have every confidence in you."

Paul watched carefully as Berry went through the same process. His eyes were not on the girl, but on the people around her. He spotted the minder, a caricature of a villain complete with dark glasses, standing at the middle part of the bar.

"You should have bet," said Berry returning to the comfort of his beer.

"I didn't want to take your money."

"That's more than can be said for your friend."

"Did you find out how much?"

"No. Looked too expensive. Why? You're not thinking of ...? You are thinking of ... Look Paul, forget it. Come on, we'll go down to Hoppe's. Maybe, Maggie and her friends will be down there."

"Yes, you're right. Just let me find out how much though. I'm curious."

"Back again?" Darting eyes and a worried look had replaced the 'welcome-the-customer' smile.

"How much?" He looked deep into those eyes and didn't see a hooker.

The smile returned, "Two thousand Euros."

"Expensive."

The smile never moved, only one eyebrow arched slightly. "For the night."

"Cash?"

"Yes."

"I don't have that sort of money at the moment."

"Goodbye."

"Look, what about tomorrow?"

"Tomorrow?"

"Tomorrow night."

"I'll be here."

"So will I. Wait for me."

All the next day, he could think of nothing else. Fortunately, the exhibition was busy, so the day passed quickly, but he made sure he got to the bank.

"I'll just collect my coat." He hadn't thought it possible, but tonight she looked even more stunning, though she wore the simplest of black dresses.

"We need to take a taxi," she said.

"Couldn't we go for a drink first?"

"We can do what ever you want after you've paid the money, and you must do that at my apartment."

The villain from the bar must have had a car nearby because, by the time they'd found a taxi, he was waiting at the apartment.

"Have a good evening," he said as he pocketed the money and left.

Paul decided to accept her offer of a drink, but refused the expensive champagne. They talked, stilted at first; he wanting to find out about her, she not wanting to reveal anything. But gradually she warmed to his charm.

An Indian father and an Arab mother had guaranteed the beauty of their daughter, Anjum. The family home was in Abu Dhabi, and there had been just enough money to send Anjum to schools in England and Switzerland. Her father's brother had a precious stone business in Amsterdam, and after visiting him several times, Anjum had liked the city enough to want to live there.

The decision to go into prostitution, two years ago, had been hers. She had always been aware of her beauty, and had thought about ways in which she could use it. She was not tall enough to be a model, and had no aptitude for acting or the hard work that went with it. She had seen how several of her uncle's business associates had been willing to lavish expensive gifts on her, just for accompanying them to various functions. Although she had never given sexual favours, she had exploited this. The step into selling her body had been a small one.

Not that she had ever walked the streets or sat in a window in Amsterdam's red-light district. From the start she had set the price high, and provided much more than a quick heavy-breathing-roll-around-the-bed.

"There it is, the story of my life," she said, but Paul sensed there was a lot more.

Anjum stood behind him and lightly touched his face with the tips of her slender fingers. "Are you feeling relaxed enough to do something else now?"

"Come and sit down. Tell me some more about growing up in Abu Dhabi."

"Whatever you want. Would you like me to get more comfortable?"

"Sit down Anjum, and you relax."

She knew he wasn't like any client she'd ever had. The look in his eyes was not lust, but something else. She hoped that she hadn't picked up her first maniac. Perhaps they'd sent him to test her.

Slowly, as the night wore on, and he talked about himself, she realised he was being completely open and sincere. As the birds began to sing he left her, his lips lightly brushing her cheek.

"Can I see you tomorrow?"

"You must have money to burn." The way he closed his eyes and took a deep breath told her these were the wrong words.

"Sunday's my day of rest." She tried to compensate by putting a degree of regret in her voice.

"Good. Maybe you can show me Amsterdam by day. Something I've not seen, despite having been here many times."

She'd suggested they meet at a canal boat departure point near to the main railway station. He'd had to work in the morning and arrived late. He almost didn't see her. She was sitting on a bench wearing a large coat with the collar turned up, and dark glasses.

She said the three-hour tour seemed like a long time, but it was one way to see everything without having to walk. They talked very little.

They had tea and small, sweet cakes in a cafe that Anjum said was off the beaten track, but worth visiting. She refused his offer to escort her back to her apartment, making some excuse about having to visit her uncle. She did accept his invitation to dinner, but only on the condition that she chose the restaurant, and that she met him there.

By the time they got to coffee, she felt herself looking at him with the same passion that radiated from his eyes.

She suggested his hotel room rather than her apartment. And, after a miniature cloak-and-dagger operation which involved them travelling in separate lifts, they fell into each other's arms as the door swung shut.

They awoke at the same time. Paul glanced at the illuminated digits; three o'clock. The tension was gone from her body, and her head lay heavily in the crook of his arm.

"You must think it's a bit strange."

"What?" he asked, sleepily.

"All this meeting in out-of-the-way places."

"Nice to see parts of a city that belong to the locals."

"There is a reason."

"Hmm."

"I didn't tell you the complete story last night."

"Hmm." He was fully awake now, but didn't want to frighten or embarrass her.

"You know what I do. I told you it was my decision to start this."

"Hmm."

"Well, now it's not my decision to continue with it."

"You want to tell me about it?"

"Yes." She spoke slowly. "Until six months ago I made a lot of money. I chose my contacts carefully, avoiding stepping on the toes of the local, organised, escort agencies. Then, one of my regular clients was found murdered. I always thought he was a respected antique shop owner, not a middleman drug trafficker. The killers found my name and telephone number in his wallet. They decided I would use my body to pay off his debt, and perhaps get them new customers for their main business of drugs."

"Why didn't you go to the police or just leave?"

"These are powerful people. They used connections in the Middle East to arrange a little car accident for my mother. Nothing too serious, a 'demonstration' they called it. Now all the money goes to them, and I receive just enough to feed and clothe myself. Even on Sunday, my day of rest, I have to be careful. They have eyes everywhere."

"What about the money you ...?"

"My immoral earnings you mean? Fortunately they are in a place where not even they can get at them."

"You can't live like this for the rest of your life."

"It might be just that."

"What do you mean?"

"One day my looks will fade, and then I'll be of no further use to them."

"And then?"

"You know nothing of this world, do you Paul? These people handle those who cross them or are no longer useful, in the same way. They remove them, permanently."

He held her close. "I won't let that happen to you."

She smiled. "You don't know what you're dealing with, Paul."

"But there must be something we can do."

"Maybe. First, I have to make sure my parents are safe, and then we'll see."

"I'll help in any way I can."

"You're not involved, Paul."

"I want to be involved. I love– "

"Shush," she said, putting her finger over his lips.

Paul's business schedule started to show many more trips via Schiphol airport. He found every excuse to visit the company's headquarters in Utrecht. They met mostly in secret on Sundays, but once in a while he paid the two thousand Euros, just in case anyone recognised his presence in Amsterdam.

Anjum never told him any details of her plans to move her parents out of reach, only that she was making progress. They fantasised about her going to England with him. For the first time in her life since she'd left the safety of her parents' home, she experienced the warm inner feeling that comes in being with someone who cares.

However, after six months, the pressures of the continual clandestine nature of their relationship began to show. For the first time, tempers started to get a little bit frayed. They didn't argue, their short times together were too precious for that, but the frustrations resulted in long periods of silence.

For two consecutive weekends, without any explanation, she told him not to come to Holland. Then, unusually, she called him on his mobile 'phone. She had something important she needed to tell him. He imagined she was going to end their relationship, and wanted to tell him to his face.

"I've been doing a lot of thinking about all the things you've said to me. I never thought I would meet someone like you, let alone someone who would tolerate this situation like you have"

"I love you."

"I know, and knowing that has played a big part in my decision."

"What decision?"

"I've decided to try to get away from here."

"How?"

"I haven't worked that out yet."

"Where to?"

"With you, to England, if you still want me."

Somehow, she'd managed to get her parents to the anonymity of London. Remarkably, they still didn't know what she did in Amsterdam; even her uncle had helped her to hide it from them.

With a heavy disguise, a false passport, an overnight bag, and the number of the bank account in Luxembourg in her head, she crossed the North Sea as a foot passenger on the Hook-of-Holland to Harwich ferry. She went to ground in a small village to the north of Norwich, which Paul had known during his University days.

They thought it was too dangerous to have any direct contact, especially as Paul was still travelling frequently to Holland. No one approached him, but he was followed on some occasions, even in England. Anjum's only contacts with the outside world were minimal visits to the village shop, and telephone calls to her parents and Paul. She always called them.

After three months they felt it was safe enough to meet in secret. They chose the Norfolk Broads, desolate in February.

The old boathouse stood on the edge of a vast expanse of water and reeds. It was only reachable down a long, single-track, private road.

As planned, Anjum arrived after Paul, having taken the bus from the village and walked. This gave her plenty of opportunity to check if either of them had been followed.

Despite the pressure of living in hiding, she seemed in a happy mood.

"I've told my parents at last what I was doing in Amsterdam."
  "How did they take it?"
"Not so well, but I hope they will grow to accept it. My father sounded very upset, and refused to speak to me any more on the telephone. I reluctantly told my mother where I would be for the next few days and gave her the telephone number here, so she can let me know how my father is reacting. If necessary I will go to see them."
"It still might be too dangerous, better to have them come to Norfolk."
"I've wanted to tell them for a long time. It was preying on my mind. Now I feel more relaxed. I can enjoy our time together. It will be like any couple having a holiday."

If only they could have been 'like any couple', thought Paul, as he lay back on the bed. He closed his eyes and tried to shut out the sound of the lapping water. But it didn't work. Every creak of the house was magnified. He even imagined he could hear the bending of the bough from which Anjum hung.
  Suddenly, a new sound dominated the others, footsteps approaching the bedroom. He felt no fear or panic as the door slowly opened.
  The man who followed the gun into the room was not the villain who'd watched over what Anjum was doing in the bar in Amsterdam. Probably not his department, thought Paul irrationally. The gun mesmerised him. As he stared at it he noticed it shaking slightly. He moved his eyes up to the face of the hired killer, and was shocked to see tears rolling down his cheeks.
  "Why couldn't you leave us alone?" Paul was surprised at how calm his voice sounded.

"She shouldn't have done it." There was genuine sadness in the man's voice.

"But it was over. Finished. She ... we just wanted to live a normal life."

"She had to pay."

"Don't you think she'd paid enough already?"

"There was no other way."

"But why hang her?"

"Tradition decides the punishment necessary."

"And you were just carrying out orders, I suppose."

"I did what had to be done."

Paul looked down at the gun again. The short barrel aimed at his chest area. "And now?" he said.

"Now, you have to die."

"Because I've seen you"

"No, because you were the one who forced Anjum down the pathway of sin."

"But that's not—" The bullet struck Paul millimetres below the heart. His head jerked to the right, and his unseeing eyes were left staring at Anjum's body.

A woman appeared in the doorway, and took the gun from the man's hands.

"Come, Bharat. You've carried out the duty demanded of you as the father of a prostitute. Our daughter and her pimp are dead."

Printed in Great Britain
by Amazon

21889991R00040